THE DOLPHIN'S DAUGHTER

GW00866729

by Alma Alexandra Hromić

Illustrated by Daniel Payne

LONGMAN

Contents

THE DOLPHIN'S DAUGHTER

THE DOLPHIN'S DAUGHTER

There was once, long ago, a land by the sea. In a castle which stood on a high rock overhanging the sea, there lived a king and a queen with an only son, a prince that would one day inherit the kingdom. As the young prince grew into manhood, the time came for him to choose a bride, but none within the borders of his kingdom suited him. So his father arranged a match with a young princess from a kingdom across the sea. Soon the matter was concluded and the bride set sail in a gilded ship from her land to come to her husband's kingdom and be wed.

The voyage was long, and often stray winds blew them off their course into strange waters, from which they then had to find their way back to their path. They saw strange golden fish that flew from the water and shone in the sunshine; once a shadow of something huge and dark passed underneath their ship, and the vessel rocked from the wake of its passing.

All was well until, almost within sight of the end of their journey, the skies darkened as though night had fallen in the middle of the day. The sun was hidden in the darkness; the wind grew stronger and stronger. It whipped and tore at the sails. A bitter rain began to fall, and the black waves broke into white foam across the ship's bows. They had brought the princess, whose name was Lilla, into her cabin for safety when the storm broke, but there was no safety to be had from that storm. Soon the wind was too strong to fight. With a sigh of surrender, the main mast of the ship gave way and split with a crack of thunder, falling like a felled tree straight down through the ship's deck and into the ocean. Water poured into the hole it had made. Still attached to the ship by the ropes and the rigging and the heavy wet remains of ragged sails, the mast, bound with bands of black iron, began to sink slowly into the ocean depths and to drag the ship under with it.

In the confusion, many tried to save their own lives, forgetting about the precious passenger who had been entrusted to their care. Sailors leaped overboard and drowned in the foaming sea. The captain and the princess's personal attendants tried to get to her to save her, but all were swept away to their own dooms by the crashing waves and the roaring wind. Princess Lilla was flung into the angry ocean clinging to a piece of battered driftwood and for a while fought to stay afloat; but soon the weight of her soaked skirts and wet hair began to pull at her with invisible fingers. Her grip on her raft began to slip. She raised her beautiful eyes to the black and purple skies, and her tears mixed with the rain on her face.

"Ah, Prince Brion!" she sighed. "I was not fated to be your bride! I go rather to the halls of the King of the Sea, to see all the drowned sailors that the sea has taken to grace his court!"

As she let go of the raft, and watched it swirl away into the oblivion of close, wet darkness, she heard a voice at her side. "Land is not far, lovely lady, and I can take you there."

"Who speaks?"

"I am Atlan," said the voice, and a huge grey dolphin swam up beside her, buoying Lilla up and refusing to let her sink. "I will save you ... but I ask a price, lovely lady."

"If I can pay it, it is yours," said Lilla.

"You will bear children," said Atlan. "Your eldest child shall be mine, the dolphin's daughter. You must bring your eldest daughter to the sea, to me, and let me take her. That is the price I ask."

Because children were far away and her own life was precious and so nearly gone, Lilla whispered, "I promise." Then she fainted away.

When she awoke, she was in a bed hung with pale blue velvet and a woman wearing a crown of gold was bending over her. "Lilla," the woman greeted her. "We were afraid we had lost you. But by a great miracle, while your ship was lost with all aboard, you were found, fainting but alive, on our beach two days ago. Luckily you were recognised from your portrait, and brought here. Now everything will be all right."

And so it was. When she recovered her strength, Lilla was wed to Brion. Within a year she reigned as Queen at King Brion's side when the old king passed away. In due time, the young Queen was brought to childbed and delivered of twin girls.

"Twins!" she thought. "That means there is no eldest daughter. The bargain is void." So she never told her husband of her miraculous survival from the shipwreck, or of its toll.

It soon became apparent that the dolphin's daughter was different from her sister. The younger twin, named Atalia, was bright and happy, with blue eyes and curly fair hair. The elder, called Delphine, was dark with huge eyes and heavy, straight black hair, and she never uttered a human sound. The King remarked on this difference before long. Lilla, who knew there was a reason behind it, was finally brought to confess her adventure in the sea. But Brion was a proud man, and unwilling to give of what was his.

"No child of mine belongs to another, whatever his claims!" Brion declared. "Whatever her faults, this is a princess of the royal line, and no daughter of a fish from the depths! Here she was born, and here she stays."

But Delphine was hard to be with, because she was always surrounded in an uncanny silence which made anyone near her uneasy and watchful. She was beautiful, in an eerie way, and her eyes were big and dark and dreamy, full of unfathomable secrets. All too soon everyone drifted away to the bright and captivating Atalia, and left the silent princess to herself. Before long, Delphine was lodged into a separate tower, which had long stood empty, right out over the emptiness of the water beneath its overhanging rock, crumbling away in places and with its own entrance through a small postern gate and a steep stair that led directly down to the sea.

The King and Queen soon forgot their oldest daughter, who lived alone but for a handful of attendants out in her tower. They had pretty Atalia to be proud of, and within three years of the birth of the twins, Queen Lilla gave birth to a son and heir to the kingdom. They called him Tarion, and the whole land celebrated his birth for a month. Tarion grew into boyhood, and by the time he was old enough to remember, his oldest sister was quite forgotten. So he grew up believing the white-and-golden Atalia to be his only sibling.

Delphine grew too, in her oblivion. She had always been striking, but she grew into a sleek and strange beauty that was quite as arresting as Atalia's much vaunted glory, although her own made no songs as her sister's did. The dolphin's daughter often came down from her tower in the early mornings, before anyone was awake, and sat watching the dawn break over the wide sea. It was as though she was waiting for something; but whatever it was, it never came.

The years passed, and the two royal sisters turned eighteen years old. Atalia had a court ball to celebrate her birthday; her sister celebrated hers alone, in the company of nobody but the few old servants assigned to her. They felt pity for the poor girl and baked her a special cake themselves, to mark the occasion as best they could. But Delphine only smiled at them with her eyes, and stroked their thin, veined old hands. In all her eighteen years she had never been heard to utter a word, although one of her servants swore that she had once heard her singing by the ocean in the early morning light – a strange, plaintive tune with no words to speak of but with a melody that broke the heart.

The ball was still going on in the early hours of the morning. The night had been still, and only gentle waves were lapping on the shingle beach below Delphine's tower when she came down to the sea in the dark hour just before dawn. The moon was full and golden, and there was a silver-sparkling path laid at Delphine's feet from the shingle beach to the distant horizon. The Princess watched it for a long time, alone, and then she stepped into the water at its beginnings. The sparkling water swirled around her feet; the moonlight dressed her hair with gold and touched her raiment with silver. She took another step, and her gown lifted and swirled around her legs. Her hair flew like a silken flag in the soft breeze. The water was around her waist, her gown a lighter billow in the darkness around her, when suddenly the silence was broken by a cry from the other end of the beach, where one of Atalia's guests must have come out to clear his head in the morning air.

"Help! There is a woman drowning! Wait, wait, I will help you!"

Delphine turned her head at the sound, and saw a tall boy of perhaps fifteen years of age, dressed in stiff court gold and brocade. He was flinging away his short cloak and racing across the shingle towards her. She had never seen her brother and did not know him; neither did he know of his hidden sister, or of the mystery of her life. All he saw was a woman in danger, and his actions were born of instinct and purity. All she saw was a bright youth rushing into danger. She raised her hands in a gesture of warding off, still silent, but it was dark and he leaped into the sea without seeing. Their common blood spoke, and she loved him for coming without question, and he would sooner have died than been thwarted in his rescue.

But there was another cry, a scream of anguish from the castle which began spilling its light and its people on to the beach. Even as it echoed out across the water, a huge wave rose above the two figures in the water and then crashed down on to the figure of the young prince, shrouding everything in a spray of foam. When the waters settled again, the Queen saw standing in the ocean a giant around whose knees the deep water swirled. In his hand was the limp body of her only son. There was nothing there to connect the giant with the dolphin who had brought her to safety many years ago to claim her crown – nothing except the darkness of his eyes, eyes which she only now really recognised as belonging to her eldest daughter: the dolphin's daughter.

"I am Atlan," said the giant. His voice shook the castle on its rock, and pieces of rubble broke off Delphine's tower and fell into the sea with white splashes. "I made a bargain with you long years ago, and even marked that which you bargained away as my own. You chose to keep what was mine. Today I exact a different price. I asked for a life; it is your choice that you paid with a death."

His fingers closed over the limp body of the prince that lay in his palm. For a while he stood there, impassive to Lilla's cries and Brion's raillery and Atalia's tears. He watched them all for a long, silent moment, and then stirred to return to his depths. The ocean whispered around his massive legs.

Then a different voice spoke. It cut through all the moans and cries and stilled everything into silence. Everyone who heard it heard it differently – some said they heard the deep and sombre darkness of the ocean's depths; other swore it was like the play of sunlight on the surface of the sea on a summer's day; still others spoke of distant and eerie melodies playing within it, like the songs of whales. But with one short word it stopped everything, and all eyes turned to the girl who had spoken – a slight, dark girl with eyes of the sea who had never spoken before in all her eighteen years.

"Wait," she said, and they all did. The giant Atlan turned to look at her, standing at his feet, looking at him with his own eyes. "I was your price," Delphine said. "And every day for years I have come to the sea's edge and waited for you to call me. Why did you not come to me then? And even now, when I had started walking to you without your call, you come in wrath to take an innocent who tried naught but to save your child from what he thought was certain death, as it would have been for any of his race? You now claim a death instead of the life that was owed you, and which has always been yours, unclaimed. So be it. But claim the death of that life, not of another's. Lay no revenge at the door of the innocents. Let my brother live; take your daughter in his place."

"It is too late," rumbled Atlan. "I took the death that was given."

"Mine is death that is given – the one you hold you stole!" said Delphine. "Father, take me – let him live."

"It was your life I wanted, beside me in the deeps," Atlan said. "Your death at my hand was never in the bargain."

"Rather at yours, who has claim, than at those of others who have no right," said Delphine.

Atlan stood in silence for a long time. Then, slowly, he stooped to lay the motionless body of Prince Tarion in the shallow water at his mother's feet. Delphine stooped over him and kissed him gently on his cool and marble-white brow, smoothing his wet hair away from his face. "Live, then, and remember me," she whispered very softly, and then turned and went willingly into Atlan's open hand. When his fingers touched her, she shivered once and then lay limp and lifeless in his huge palm. At the same time, Tarion shuddered where he lay, and drew a shallow breath. They all bent over to succour him, and so none but Tarion himself, whose eyes opened and looked past the crowds of those who would aid him on to the sea, saw the first touch of dawn on the waters. In silence so total it was deafening to Tarion's ear, the young prince saw the giant Atlan raise his eyes to the sky and open his mouth in a silent scream of anguish, and then fall, a wall of sparkling, disembodied foam, into the waters of his birth.

"Look," somebody called out, "the Princess! The Princess!"

Tarion sat up and looked where they had pointed. He saw lying in the shallows of the beach the body of the dark and lovely young woman whom he had tried to save from drowning only moments before. Her eyes were closed and she was smiling.

"Who was she?" the young Prince cried.

"The dolphin's daughter," said someone.

And so she remained. Royal she might have been, but over his priests in matters ecclesiastical her father had no rule, and because of her end none would bury her in sacred ground. She was laid in a distant grave, close to the sea; and often from it the people who passed near swore they heard plaintive song. Above her grave a tree grew, a tree the like of which grew nowhere else in the land. It had a fruit that grew the colour of the eyes of Atlan, and it tasted of the ocean, or of tears.

My music was my life, my life my music

My Music Was My Life, My Life My Music

The old forest knew Niklas. He would come wandering along the shadowed paths playing his nut-brown fiddle, and the leaves on the trees would dance for the joy of his music. The stags would come to the edge of the paths to watch him go by, and the rabbits played leapfrog to his rhythms in the long grass of the clearings. Birds knew his tunes, and would sing along. Music always followed in Niklas' wake. He lived for the music, and the music came tremblingly alive for him, pouring from under his bow, wrapping the frets of his violin, making the forest laugh and lilt.

The fiddle had been a gift from his grandmother for Niklas' thirteenth birthday. The two of them lived alone in a cottage deep in the woods. Niklas had never seen either his father or his mother. Grandmother would say nothing about the gift except that it had always belonged to the family, and was very old – and that it had been left for him to have when the time came. It seemed to be a magic fiddle because it seemed to teach Niklas how to play it, guided his fingers to play the right notes. The first time he held it in his hands he could play any tune he wanted. It was as though playing the fiddle was something he had always known how to do, and had merely remembered something that he had forgotten. So taken was he by his gift that he did not see his grandmother weep when she saw what had happened, and did not ask her why she was crying.

Niklas had been admonished not to leave the forest where he lived. Once he had asked his grandmother, when he was still very young, if the forest covered the whole world. She could have told him then that it did. But she had sighed, sat him down, and explained that there was a whole wide world outside the forest. That had been only the first time that she had told him that he must never enter it. There had never come another day when she did not repeat those words to Niklas. And, because he was happy, he did not wish to disobey her. The world held no call for him. He was happy to roam his forest home with his fiddle. The beasts all knew him and came to him if he called to them. He could make the tiny wild flowers in the clearings sway to his music like graceful, little dancers. He could make the nightingales sing for him. He was king of his kingdom. He was happy.

One day he was sitting on the low bough of a favourite oak tree and playing his fiddle when he heard an unfamiliar sound. He stopped playing to listen and soon the noise grew closer. Along the path that meandered beneath his swinging feet a procession of riders came slowly, weaving their way through the woods. There was an expression of fear on the lead rider's face, and he kept making strange signals with his hand, as though warding away evil spells. Behind him, on a milk-white palfrey, rode the most beautiful girl Niklas had ever seen. She had long golden hair that streamed like sunshine down her shoulders, and she had the eyes of a fawn. She didn't seem as afraid as her escort, because she was smiling as she looked around her. She was humming a tune, very softly, under her breath. Niklas listened intently for a moment and then, carried away with the girl's beauty, his fiddle seemed to leap into his hands and he played an echo of the tune she was humming. Instantly the cavalcade came to a milling halt beneath him, and scared voices were raised in raucous query. The girl looked immediately up to where he was sitting, and smiled.

"Why, hello," she said. "That was well played. What are you doing here all alone?"

"Playing the fiddle," said Niklas.

"Come down! Come down here at once! Are you alone? Where are your parents?" chattered the lead rider, quite pale, but recovering. "Where did you come from anyway? What is a youngster like you doing in the Enchanted Forest on his own? Who sent you here?"

"I live here," said Niklas, "with my grandmother."

"But nobody lives here," said the girl reasonably. "This is the Enchanted Forest."

"I do, I live here. Where are you from? Where are you going? I have never seen anyone pass this way before."

"I am ..." she began, but the lead rider leaned over to clutch at her arm.

"Princess!" he remonstrated urgently.

"He is only a child, Ilon!" she said, shaking him off. "I am Princess Briagha. I come from my father's house, to marry Prince Balach. I go to my wedding, forest boy."

Niklas laughed, and played a snatch of a happy tune on his fiddle. "Luck to you then!" he said, and laughed again. He played faster and faster, and soon the fear on everyone's faces began to melt as the smiles came. The princess clapped her hands in time to his music and laughed joyously. Even dour Ilon was surprised into a smile. When Niklas stopped, breathless, Princess Briagha held out her hands to him.

"Oh please come and play at my wedding, forest boy! You make such happy music, and I know that my betrothed will welcome you, as I do!"

Niklas laughed out loud and leapt down from his perch on the tree. Such was his joy at having been asked by this beautiful girl to play his music at her wedding feast that he quite forgot his grandmother's constant words of warning.

"You can ride behind Ban," said Princess Briagha. A handsome young man swept off his plumed hat and laughed down at Niklas. The knight leaned down from his mount and help Niklas clamber up behind him, his fiddle tucked between them. Then Ilon gave the signal and they moved off. The Princess rode beside Ban and Niklas, and talked happily about her wedding; Niklas listened avidly and it was only when he felt the sunshine hot on his bare head that he turned and saw the edge of the Enchanted Forest being relentlessly left behind. For an instant his grandmother's voice came to him, and her words about the forest returned to touch his mind. He shivered where he sat with a sense of doom, knowing, for just an instant, that he had done something irrevocable. But then Briagha's lilting laugh drew him back, and he turned his back on the forest. Somewhere far ahead he thought he could see a castle of many turrets, each flying a white pennant to welcome the new bride. And soon he would be playing at a royal wedding.

In the joyous chaos of their arrival at Prince Balach's castle, Niklas somehow seemed to be left behind in the throng. The cooks fed him because he came in with the princess and they assumed that he belonged to her. But he could not ever get close to her again, for she was always surrounded by throngs of other, more important people. Once he saw her walking with Prince Balach and came to bow to her, but she was laughing up into her prince's eyes and did not see him. Prince Balach merely swept past him with haughty eyes. Niklas retreated and watched from a distance. It was not his lot to be numbered into the friends of the princely pair. The day of the nuptials was drawing near; then, surely, Briagha would remember her strange troubadour.

In his innocence, Niklas had thought that he was to have been the only player at their feast. He stood in the decked hall with his violin and surveyed the throngs of musicians and singers that milled about waiting their turn. If it had been within his power, Niklas would have turned and run all the way back to the Enchanted Forest, where he was loved and where his music was eagerly awaited. But once again he was stayed by the sight of the princess, more beautiful than ever in her wedding gown. Surely she would remember him when the time came? Niklas found himself an unobtrusive place in the musicians' gallery, and settled down to wait.

Course after course of the wedding feast was served, and the music poured from the musicians' gallery like silver waterfalls. When one group stopped, another began, and they in their turn were succeeded by others. Niklas waited, silent. He waited for a moment of silence when he would be called to play. But the moment never came, and the feast was already drawing to a close. Niklas' eyes filled with tears because he finally knew that he had been a whim, chosen and then forgotten. Uncalled, his violin leapt into his hands and he began playing, very softly, a quiet melody. At first nobody heard him over all the din, but soon the other musicians began to, and one by one the other instruments stopped. In the spreading silence from the musicians' gallery, the laughter and chatter in the hall began to still as the notes of Niklas' violin came sweeping down to them, suddenly filled with power. They carried a different message to

all who heard him play, and Briagha was not the only one who
wept behind her hands. Niklas, seeing her weep, was moved
once again by her beauty and the violin changed its tune. Soon
he had the entire hall clapping their hands and stamping their
feet, and the royal couple were laughing with joy at one another
and dancing in the midst of the hall.

Eventually Niklas' violin died slowly away and his hands
dropped from the magical instrument, exhausted. There was a
moment of silence while the guests realised that the music was
over. Then the rafters shook with their cheers and their
clapping. They brought Niklas down from the gallery and set
the finest of wines before him. Briagha herself sat beside him
and fed him from her own plate.

"How handsome the lad is," the people murmured to
themselves, seeing him sitting there. "And such golden hands.
Surely there can be no better fiddler in the world!"

When he was finally escorted, transported beyond happiness
by the acclamation he had gathered at Briagha's wedding, to his
new chambers high up in the towers and close to Briagha's own,
Niklas saw his reflection in a polished shield that hung on his
wall. He was no longer the boy who had left the Enchanted
Forest only days ago. He was taller by a head, more; he had the
rangy body of an adolescent and no longer the small, round,
smiling face of the boy from the Enchanted Forest. His fingers
were longer and stronger, and on his upper lip was the first faint
shadow of down. Thus Niklas at least understood the price he
had paid for trespassing beyond the borders of his forest. He
would know adulation and fame; but he would never again have
immortality.

He stayed at Balach and Briagha's court for some time, their treasure and their pride; but he did not play often, and it was soon obvious that he aged a little every time he did. After a while, Niklas slipped out one day and walked away. He did not look back. He did not know that he was missed and looked for; but that all too soon he was put aside and replaced by newer entertainments. The name of Niklas the Fiddler became a tale.

Niklas travelled the world, playing the fiddle when he needed money to survive, and every time he played he aged a little more. In the space of a few years he had gone through adolescence into middle age; in a few more, he was an old man. Soon the fiddle was put away, for Niklas feared that he would carry himself beyond the last boundary. There was one thing he wanted to do before he laid down his charmed life. He wanted to go home. If the price of his final melody was to be his life, he wanted to play it beneath the eaves of the Enchanted Forest.

His travels took him, now a stooped and white-haired old man, past the castle where once he had played at a wedding feast. He knew he ought to have walked straight past and turned his back on the castle walls where he had known such bitter sorrow before he had known joy. But it was stronger than him. He walked inside and asked to see the prince.

"The Prince, forsooth," said one of the knights in the entrance hall. "Do you think we allow every vagabond off the street to see the Prince? The Prince has better things to do."

"But he will want to see me," Niklas said, "he or Princess Briagha. Yes, she will remember me. It was she who brought me from the forest, a little gypsy boy, to play at their wedding feast. I would like to play for her once again."

"Liar," said another knight. "I was at their wedding feast. The gypsy who played for them was young, merely a boy. It has only

been a few years since they were wed; the gypsy boy could not have become a grandfather in that time."

"Please," said Niklas. "My music is my life, my life my music. Both are drawing to a close. Let me play for my beautiful princess once more."

"Listen," said another voice. Niklas turned, recognising it for that of Ban, who once carried him to this castle on his own horse. But Ban showed no recognition, and he had not been speaking to him but to the other knights. "The old man wants to entertain us. Well, would you like to see an entertainment? I will throw him out myself. Come!"

Niklas started to speak, but Ban picked him up and carried him through the oaken gates into the courtyard, pitching him outside into the horse-churned mud beside the main paved roadway. He stood on the top step of the castle entrance, his hands on his hips. Behind him crowded the other knights. They were all laughing.

"Play, old man!" Ban called. "Play for Princess Briagha now!"

Niklas picked himself up painfully and dragged himself out of the outer gates, the knights' laughter following behind him. He glanced up once as he walked away. Ghostly white pennants seemed to fly from the battlements, as a different, kinder laughter flooded the courtyard in his memory. But then the pennants were gone, and he knew he would never hear Briagha laugh again. He hunched his shoulders against the cold and began shuffling slowly in the direction of the forest.

He had nothing to eat or drink, but something gave him strength to continue even when everything seemed lost. It was almost beyond his belief when he looked up and realised that the first branches of the Enchanted Forest were spreading over his head. He wept when he saw them, recalling the days of his innocence in their shadow. He moved in deeper, deeper, until he could move no longer and simply sat down beneath an ancient oak. He drew out his violin and looked at it for a long time, his tears flowing freely; then he slowly lifted it up on his shoulder and laid his chin on the place it had worn smooth so many years ago. His hand was shaking as he laid the bow upon the strings. He should have played false, his notes trembling out of true and discords marring the forest's peace. But the violin burst forth into a bubbling melody that flowed into the trees, seemingly unguided by Niklas' hands, finally asking the question as to who was the player and who the played.

The stags heard the air and lifted their heads in wonder. The rabbits and the foxes pricked their ears. The flowers in the clearing, beginning to fade as the autumn set in, allowed the last of their summer colour to blaze out as they began swaying in a dance they had almost forgotten. Somewhere deep in the forest, an echo reached the cottage where Niklas' grandmother still dwelt in the forest peace and she stood quite still for a moment before reaching for her shawl and hurrying, led by an unerring instinct, towards the clearing where Niklas was playing his violin. The song had a name, and the name was woven of the words he himself had spoken in the castle courtyard to a jeering crowd: *my music is my life, my life my music.* Both were ebbing away, the melody dying on a high, sobbing note that only a violin can draw out from within the depths of a soul before flowing into a reverent silence made poignant by the absence of sound.

Niklas was dead by the time his grandmother reached him, his violin broken in two by his side. In the silence he was surrounded by the beasts who had loved him, and who were the only ones to grieve over his passing. His grandmother wept over the frail old man, for she knew of his journeys, his seeking and the love that had destroyed him in the end. She raised a cairn over him where he had sat down to play his last air, over him and over the broken violin. And a new spell was woven about the Enchanted Forest. For the infrequent travellers who chanced its perilous paths now came out telling of a cairn in a clearing, the occasionally-glimpsed wraith of a small, dark-skinned boy and a strange melody which now hung in the shadows between the trees, its sad refrain repeating the same few sorrowful words: *My music was my life, my life my music.*

THE PERFECT ROSE

THE PERFECT ROSE

There lived once in a land far away to the East, so far that it sat right under the sun when it rose every morning, a great king. He was a good king, a wise and powerful one; he was young and strong, and he loved his people, and they him.

There came a time for the King to choose a bride, and ambassadors from many lands flocked to his city, each extolling the princess of his own country. But when the princesses arrived for him to choose, he looked at them all and immediately pointed to a very dark and very lovely princess from a land close to his own borders.

"She and no other will be my Queen!" he vowed.

So the wedding was celebrated; the people rejoiced and threw rose petals and flowers of jasmine before her whenever she passed by. She smiled at them with her little, rosebud mouth and out of her slanting, dark eyes. She waved with a dainty, little hand, and her wrists were heavy with the gold and jewelled bracelets the King had given her to prove his love for her.

Now the King had a rose garden in the grounds of his palace, hidden from all eyes by a high wall. He loved this garden, and was proud of it. He often walked in it, along paths bordered by red, white and yellow roses, enjoying the fragrance that perfumed the air. Nobody else ever went there, not even the Queen. Never were the roses cut from the trees while still in bloom, but only when they were dry and ugly; then the King himself would cut them and take them away. No one ever saw the roses except the King; it was his only selfishness in life, the only thing he did not share even with his dearly beloved Queen.

She, a spoiled princess who had become a pampered queen, grew more and more jealous of the Rose Garden. She even began to think that the King went there to meet another woman, whose eyes then saw what her own were denied. Her hate grew and festered because she never spoke of it to anybody. She became determined to see what she was forbidden to look upon. She made plans.

Then suddenly the Queen took to her bed one day with an inexplicable malady. It left her cheeks pale and her eyes dull, and she neither spoke nor smiled. The King, afraid for her life, sent all over his land for the best physicians he knew. They all went away from the Queen's bedside saying that they knew not what ailed her, and that none of their remedies had worked a cure.

So the King sent them away and tended her himself. For seven days and nights he sat by her. She neither moved nor spoke; but he did not sleep because he wanted to be there if she needed him.

Finally, on the eighth evening, she turned to him and whispered, "My Lord, why sittest thou there by the foot of my bed?"

"Because thou hast been ill, and I have tended thee. The physicians could not cure thee, and nobody knows what ails thee. Tell me, for if there is something that will make thee well, I shall do it myself."

"There is something, Lord," she said, and in her eyes there was a gleam of triumph and of malice. But he saw them not, saw only her.

"Speak!" he cried.

She said, "I want the most perfect rose from thy Rose Garden."

The King frowned and drew back. He said, "If that is the only thing that will heal thee, then I shall find it. But my heart is troubled."

"It is the only thing," she said.

So he rose and went out into the garden. The moon was full, the garden full of light and all the roses seemed perfect to him. He wandered for a long time, and finally cut the topmost bud from the youngest and loveliest rose tree. The night dew was still upon the bud, sparkling like diamonds and the white petals looked like wrought silver beneath it. The King took up the rose and went into the Queen's bedchamber. "Look!" he said. "I have brought it. Here is the loveliest rose from my garden. Now, beloved, let the roses return to thine own cheeks, and thy sickness lift."

But the Queen looked on the rose and laughed. "Is that the best thou canst do?" she said. "Thy garden is no marvel then; but I have heard told of a magic garden of roses, to be found further East still than thy kingdom. *There* grows the most perfect rose in all the world. There must thou go; and that rose must thou bring before me. Otherwise I shall surely die."

So the King took the white rose away, for the Queen would have none of it, and placed it into his own bosom. He ordered his horse to be saddled and rode off from his kingdom with a heavy heart to search for the perfect rose for his Queen.

He rode a long way; he passed the borders of his own country and entered a burning desert. It seemed to have no end, but stretched out all around him. He travelled in it for many days. Soon the day came when he had no water left to drink. He had seen no trace of it in the land he travelled. He sat down in the meagre shadow of a squat cactus, to at least partly shield himself from the merciless sun. His horse stood beside him on trembling legs and the King could not meet the animal's patient, pain-filled eyes. He buried his head in his hands in despair. It was then that he heard a soft voice, like the chiming of a thousand little bells. The voice spoke to him: "Be not afraid, O King, but take thy rose from thy bosom and take what it gives thee."

So the King reached for the white rose and there on its petals still shimmered the night dew that had fallen on them many nights ago in his garden. Wonderingly, the King shook the drops of water on to his palm and a little water collected there. It was not much, just a thin film of moisture, but the King offered it first to his horse. The animal licked off the water, but now looked at its master even more mournfully than before. The King said, "Look! It was only the dew from the rose – and I have no more to give."

But as he looked on the rose he saw that there were still dewdrops on it, and he thought that now there were more than before. So he shook them off again and the more he shook, the more there was, until both horse and man were satisfied. The King put the rose carefully back into his bosom and went on his way.

There came a time when the King and his horse shared out the last morsel of the food they had brought. Once more the King despaired. Again the voice like the chiming of a thousand bells spoke to him. "Be not afraid, O King, but take thy rose from thy bosom and take what it gives thee."

So the King took out the rose again. He marvelled at how fresh and lovely the flower still was even after many days in the searing desert heat. He plucked off a velvet-soft white petal because it seemed the right thing to do, but he did not do it gladly, for it marred the rose. Even as he looked the rose was as before, and still he held the petal in his hand. He put the rose back into the folds of his garments and laid the petal down on the hot sand. The petal began to grow and grow. It grew until it lay at the King's feet as a cloth of the finest white silk. Then the cloth brought forth food – a feast fit for an emperor.

When both horse and man were satisfied, the sumptuous dishes vanished and the cloth became once more a rose petal. The King gathered it up with care and placed it next to the rose from which it had been plucked.

And so the King journeyed on. When he needed water, he drank the dew from the rose; when he hungered, he ate from the cloth that the rose had spread before him. The rose never faded, but was ever as fresh as on the day it had been plucked and always as white as snow.

The King journeyed ever East, always searching for the fabulous garden of his Queen's vision. He passed through many cities and asked many people, but they all knew nothing. Some said they knew of it, but that it lay further East still – the next city, the next realm. And so he travelled on.

He came to a great sea, and knew not how to cross it. The shores were deserted. They stretched out to his left and his right so that he could see no end to them. There was not even a fisherman's hut where he could find a boat to take him across. He gazed at the foam of salt water which swirled around his feet and thought sadly that this must be where his journey ended.

But again he heard the small voice like the chiming of a thousand bells, and it said, "Be not afraid, O King, but take thy rose from thy bosom and take what it gives thee."

So the King took out the white rose again. He plucked another petal and let it float on the foam of the water. It grew and grew, and became a boat of the finest, lightest, polished white wood, the like of which he had never seen before. He stepped on board, leading his horse, for there was easily room for both. The boat, which sailed by itself with no sailor to tend it, reared up delicate white sails of silk and turned into the wind.

For many days the King sailed in the petal boat, for the sea was a wide one to cross. At length, he glimpsed the shadow of land on the horizon. He shouted with joy as he looked on it for the voyage across the waters had been lonely and he rejoiced that he would soon see people again.

The boat came ashore quietly on an empty beach of white sand. It then became once again a single white rose petal floating on the even whiter foam of the sea. The King scooped it up lovingly and placed it with the rose again. Then he was riding once again. Presently he began to look at the land around him, first with puzzlement and then with a growing joy, for it was his own country that he was riding through. But when he looked closer, his eyes clouded with pain and anger. His fertile land was a tangle of wild bushes and weeds; the neat little houses of his people were dirty and ruinous; thin and mangy dogs scavenged there and quarrelled over what meagre food they found. The further he rode, the worse it became; even the great, wide road he had been travelling on fell into disrepair. Grass grew on it and around it, and thorn bushes crowded in and scratched at his legs and the flanks of his horse if he went too near. The King

rode on with a sorely troubled heart and lamented the day he had left on his quest, for it seemed that the land had been ruled most evilly in his absence and the glory of his kingdom was forgotten.

He wept when he saw the city walls. The city that had once been the most beautiful in all the kingdoms was now mean and sly. Little, rat-like people scurried from one corner to the next and stared at the golden clasp on the King's cloak with avarice shining palely from their eyes.

"Where are all the people?" the King asked one. "Where is your Queen?" he asked another, and "Where is your King, and what city is this now?" he asked of a third.

"We are the people, there are no other," said the first; "We have no Queen," said the second; "We have no King," said the third, "although it is said we once had one. This is no city. These are but walls we live in, for safety's sake."

The King pointed at the ruined wall that he knew had once been his palace, and asked a fourth man, "What is that up there?"

The man replied, "It is nothing now. I have heard it said that it was once a great palace. Nobody goes there now, but I have heard it said that somewhere within there is a magic rose garden in which there grows the most perfect rose in all the world."

"So," said the King, "I have come to the end of my journey and it is at the place of its beginning."

He urged his horse towards the Garden, his Garden, the Garden of the Perfect Rose.

When he got to the palace, he saw that it really was no more. Rooms lay open to the sky, mildew had eaten the gold-embroidered tapestries and cobwebs had taken their places.

Where once carpets from Persia spread their luxurious tread, there now grew grass and small field flowers, no less lovely for their humbler beginnings. Where spirited horses had lived in gold-embossed stables, now mice and rats scurried and rustled in the rotting straw.

The palace was the King's no more. It had a different ruler now, for Nature had taken what she could and left what she could not touch to Decay, with whom she shared her throne.

The King walked through the familiar corridors. They echoed around him, hollow, empty. At length he reached the little door under the archway, the door that led to the garden. He took the key from where it hung around his neck on a silken cord and put it into the keyhole. At first it wouldn't turn; the years that had gone by had taken their toll even on the locked and untouched gate. But then, slowly and creakily, it gave. The door swung inward on complaining hinges. And lo! Out of the whole palace the garden alone was as it had been, fresh and pure and lovely, and the same haunting scent of roses hung lightly in the air. Nobody had been inside that garden – not through that stiff and time-frozen door – yet there were no dead blooms on the rose trees, no dead twigs; they had been watered, the weeds had been pulled and the pathways tended. The King stood in the doorway and looked on in wonder, for he could not understand how these things could have been done.

Then he shut the door behind him and walked over to the high eastern wall of the Garden and opened a little hidden window in the wall. He opened the window, and once more he wept, for out of that window he could see all too clearly the sordid alleys of his city that once had been so beautiful and the shabbiness of the countryside all around. He wept at the way the shine of glory had gone from his kingdom. The people had to live under this gloom – and he, their king, could do nothing because his people would no longer believe that he existed.

Then he heard the soft voice like the chiming of a thousand bells, and it said to him, "Be not afraid, O King, but take thy rose from thy bosom and take what it gives thee."

The King did this, but he looked at the rose sorrowfully and said, "Alas, my faithful companion, I believe the remedy of this situation will tax even thy powers. For what canst thou do against fear and greed and disbelief? What canst thou do to restore the people to what they once were?"

And the voice spoke again: "It is the last thing I can do for thee, O King; I will cure thy kingdom."

"I did not know thou couldst talk!" exclaimed the King in surprise.

"Thou didst not ask."

"Then the stories are true," said the King, "for I do indeed hold in my hand the most perfect rose that ever was."

"Nay," said the rose, "that one was beyond thy powers to find. But here, within thy world, perhaps thou dost speak truly."

"Then why didst thou not tell me? For had I known, I would never have gone on this quest, and my kingdom would still be whole."

"Thou didst know. Why else wouldst thou have picked from the rose tree thou chose? It was thy wife who made thee believe otherwise; she knew not perfection when she saw it and she laughed at it. So she drove it away, and thy kingdom wilted under her cruel hand."

"If I had known ..."

"Thou didst know. Only thy love was too strong. Thou hast

held the perfection of thy kingdom all this time safe next to thy heart. Thy love was worthy, King; thy Beloved was not. Therefore thou hadst to leave, before she destroyed thee."

The King bowed his head, and was silent for a long time.

The White Rose presently rustled again and the voice like the chiming of a thousand little bells spoke once more. "If thou dost want thy kingdom back, then hearken. Pluck four petals, each with a drop of dew, and release each into a wind from a different corner of the world."

So the King did as he was bid. He plucked the four petals with dew on them from the White Rose, and the Winds swirled around his head. First came the North Wind, sullen and cold; he snatched the petal offered him and disappeared into the distance amid a great howling and moaning. The West Wind followed his brother, salty from the sea from which he hied. He murmured an apology for his brother from the North, for the West Wind was the peacemaker. With a word of welcome, he also took up his petal and flew away. The East Wind arrived next, with sand from her deserts swirling around her skirts; her breath was hot and dry, and she curled the petal protectively around its dew so as not to harm it. She, too, offered a welcome before departing. Lastly it was the turn of the South Wind, her breath sweet with the scent of frangipani and jasmine from the isles of the South. She took up her petal as gently as a mother would her babe, promised she would deliver it well, and planted a light, feathery kiss on the King's brow – then she, too, was gone. The voice of a thousand chiming bells spoke softly and it seemed to the King to be faint and very far away. "Turn thy eyes outward, O King, and behold."

The King did. As he watched, he understood how the Rose Garden had kept itself tended so well. For where the dew of the White Rose fell, the same dew that had quenched his thirst in the wilderness, all that was evil or foul melted away and there arose the cleanliness and love and faith that had succoured his kingdom before the evil times had come. Whichever side he looked, it was the same picture – the land was coming back to life, and his people with it. The King wept once again, but this time it was for joy.

But when he looked down at the rose in his hands, he saw that it had taken on the colour of cold ashes, and the smooth petals had shrivelled into wrinkles and lines. And he exclaimed, "Thou art dying! What can I do to aid thee?"

"The new glory of thy kingdom will never fade, for it is the glory of the heart of the rose. From this moment, thy kingdom will be thy garden; but this garden will not bloom again – it will die, for it has given its heart away in four drops of its dew. I, too, must die with it. Farewell, O King. Thy garden has repaid thy love."

When the King looked again, he held naught but a handful of fine ash dust, and when he turned to look at the lovely rose garden he had entered only a short time ago, all he saw was a waste – a graveyard of dry and dead rose trees. Around each, on the earth by its roots, lay a pale wreath of dust which had been its leaves and flowers.

The King came out of the dead garden, his heart heavy with sorrow. The people, his people, such as he remembered them, came and thronged around him and shouted welcome from a thousand throats. The King said to them, "Peace! Be still, there is a tale I have to tell you."

So they fell quiet and listened as he related the history of the rose, and they were silent for a long time when he had finished speaking. Then the King asked after the finest gold and silversmiths in the city, and the finest makers of gems, and they came forward. To the goldsmith he said, "You will coat all the rose trees in the garden with the finest gold you can find, and fashion blossoms of red and yellow gold to adorn their branches forever."

To the silversmith he said, "You will make a White Rose out of the most fragile and precious silver."

"And you," he said to the maker of gems, "will form crystal dew drops out of the most perfect diamonds, and adorn the rose of silver with them."

"This rose," he then said, "will be placed upon the topmost tip of the rose bush which I shall show you. The Perfect Rose will bloom forever in the Garden it has made its own."

As he said, so it was done. The voice like the chiming of a thousand little bells may be silent, but the beauty of the White Rose, the most perfect rose that ever was, will never pass away.